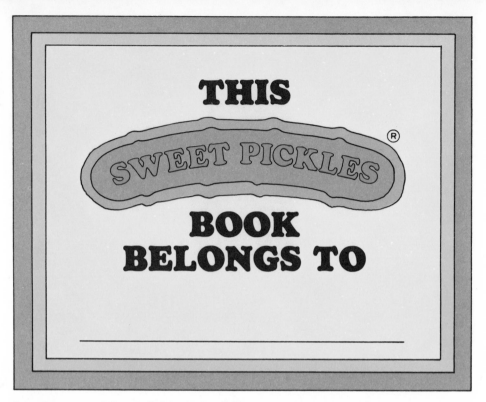

THIS

SWEET PICKLES ®

BOOK
BELONGS TO

_____

In the world of *Sweet Pickles,* each animal gets into a pickle because of an all too human personality trait.

This book is about Yakety Yak who talks and never listens.

Other Books in the Sweet Pickles Series

WHO STOLE ALLIGATOR'S SHOE?
FIXED BY CAMEL
ELEPHANT EATS THE PROFITS
GOOSE GOOFS OFF
ME TOO IGUANA
LION IS DOWN IN THE DUMPS
MOODY MOOSE BUTTONS
QUAIL CAN'T DECIDE
STORK SPILLS THE BEANS
VERY WORRIED WALRUS
ZIP GOES ZEBRA

Library of Congress Cataloging in Publication Data

Hefter, Richard.
  Yakety yak yak Yak.

  (Sweet Pickles series)
  SUMMARY: Yak drives everybody crazy with his
incessant talking, until he drives his taxi right
into a big hole.
  [1. Yaks—Fiction] I. Title. II. Series.
PZ7.H3587Yak   [E]   77-7250
ISBN 0-03-021436-X

Printed in the United States of America

Weekly Reader Books' Edition

Weekly Reader Books presents

YAKETY YAK YAK YAK

Written and Illustrated
by Richard Hefter
Edited by Ruth Lerner Perle

Holt, Rinehart and Winston · New York

Walrus was riding in Yak's taxi. "Listen to me, Yak," he moaned. "This is important!"

"Important," said Yak. "You want to hear about something important? I'll tell you about something important."

"Yak, stop!" groaned Walrus.

"Why, just yesterday," continued Yak, "I was talking to Stork and he said the same thing. Everybody says that to me. 'Listen,' they say, or, 'Stop talking,' they say. Well, I just think they're rude. And I say, "If you can't wait to hear a person out and feel you have to interrupt all the time, it's just not polite.' Let me tell you what Camel did today…"

"But, Yak!" wailed Walrus.

"…Camel was just standing there, shouting *Taxi! Taxi!* What a silly thing to yell! Anyone can see I'm in a taxi," continued Yak. "Why else would I have a sign on my roof that says *TAXI?* It says *TAXI,* and that's just what it is. So when anyone calls *Taxi! Taxi!* I stop. 'Yak's Taxi Service,' I say. 'That's me. No job too small. We go anywhere. Service with a smile. Out-of-town rates cheerfully given. We get you where you want to go. Leave the driving to Yak.' That's what I told Camel."

"BUT YAK…!" cried Walrus. "I have to tell you something, please listen."

"…Then, when Camel got in, she said, 'Stop talking and take me to the garage. My truck is broken.' *Stop talking!* she said. I mean, *really*. Imagine that… telling me to stop talking!"

"BUT YAK…!" yelled Walrus.

"…And furthermore, everyone knows I never refuse a passenger, not even Nightingale…and you know what she's like. And I certainly wouldn't refuse Camel, especially when her truck is broken down and she has to get to the garage. No sir, cheerful service, that's my motto. And another thing…"

"Please, Yak," sighed Walrus. "We just passed my house again. For the fourth time. You keep driving around and around the block, and I'm getting dizzy. Please let me out."

"What?" said Yak. "Passed your house? Well, why didn't you say something? You have to learn to speak up, Walrus. You can't go around worrying so much. It's not good for you. It can make you dizzy."

"But, Yak...!" said Walrus.

"Well, I'm sorry, Walrus, old pal," said Yak, "but I can't sit around all day listening to your troubles. I have to earn a living. Got to get over to the bank and pick up Rabbit. He gets downright testy if I'm late."

"Good-bye, Yak," said Walrus.
Yak drove off.

When Yak pulled up in front of the bank, Rabbit
was waiting.

"You are eleven minutes late," said Rabbit, looking
at his watch.

"I knew it," said Yak. "Eleven silly minutes and you
are making a big fuss."

"I only mentioned it," said Rabbit, "because…"

"Rush, rush, rush," complained Yak. "Everybody is always in such a big hurry. No time for anything important anymore. 'Where's the fire?' I say. 'Why all the hustle and bustle?' I said that to Quail on Tuesday, and do you know what she said? She said, 'I'm not sure.' Now I ask you! What kind of an answer is that? Nobody's sure anymore. That's the problem."

"Yak," said Rabbit, "that sign said *Road Closed.*"

"...And that's not the only problem," said Yak. "Just look around you. Everybody has problems. Too much, not enough, it's all the same. I was just telling Walrus about what Camel said to me today."

"Yak," said Rabbit, "this road is definitely closed for a reason."

"Camel just stood there, waving her arms and shouting *Taxi! Taxi!*" continued Yak. "And when she finally got in the taxi, she told me to stop talking. Imagine that! 'Stop talking,' she says to me. Folks are always telling me that. I don't understand it. Anyone can see that I am most agreeable and that I like a good conversation. I'm not picky. I'll talk to anybody, even Nightingale…and you know what she's like!"

"I'll tell you what's bothering me," said Rabbit.

"See what I mean?" said Yak.

"You have just driven this taxi into a hole," said Rabbit.

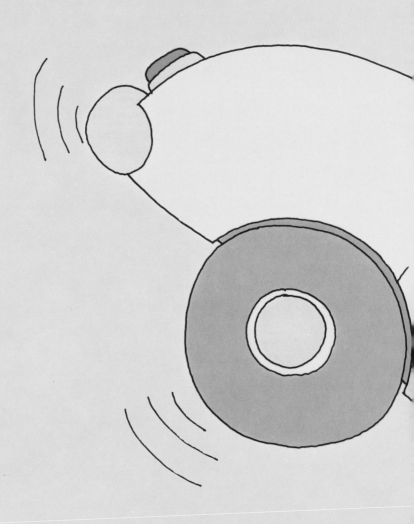

"It really is interesting to find out about the kinds of things that bother people," said Yak. "This morning, Walrus was really dizzy and I figure that he worries too much and that's what causes these dizzy spells and that...hey, Rabbit, where are you going?"

"...And that's the big trouble with everyone today. They're all in a hurry. Rush, rush, rush. Nobody has time to listen anymore. Listen, did I tell you about Walrus' dizzy spells. It really is serious...!"

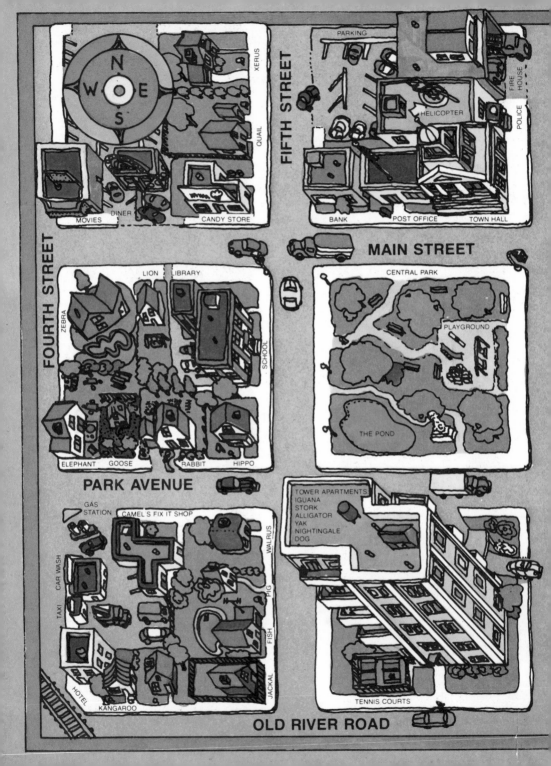